I Met a MAN

John Ciardi

Illustrated by Robert Osborn

HOUGHTON MIFFLIN COMPANY BOSTON

ISBN: 0-395-06695-6 HARDBOUND
ISBN: 0-395-17447-3 PAPERBOUND

First Printing C

This book is for JONNEL *because he helped me with it, because he has learned*

.

CONTENTS

to read it, and because he and Myra and Benn and I have had such fun with it.

THESE POEMS were written for a special pleasure: I wanted to write the first book my daughter read herself. To bring them within her first-grade range, I based them on the two most elementary word lists in general use. Those word lists contain a total of slightly more than four hundred words. The word lists themselves, however, are obviously designed as a measure of minimum accomplishment for a first grader: they in no way measure the real reading accomplishment of a bright child.

Such a child, moreover, is bound to find a special pleasure in being led to recognize new words without outside help. Poetry is especially well designed to lead the child to such recognition, for rhyme and pattern are always important clues.

I decided, therefore, to use the basic lists not as an absolute limit, but as a way of getting the beginning reader on the page by using a vocabulary that would be largely familiar. With that assurance and with the bribe of pleasure that is the reward of poetry, the child will certainly be able not only to recognize the words in which he has been drilled in the first-grade class, but to figure out new words.

The basic devices of these poems for leading the child to new words are rhyme, riddles, context, and word games. The point of the riddles, as far as learning is concerned, is that the child will be able to guess the word even without seeing it written. When he does see it written, therefore, he will know what it is no matter how difficult it may be in terms of graduated word lists.

Since my object was not only to engage the basic first-grade word list but to lead the child beyond it, I have gradually introduced slightly more difficult words into the poems. Almost any child halfway through the first grade should be able to read the first poems. Any bright child toward the end of the first grade should be able to solve the slight added difficulties of the later poems. Certainly there is no reason to shun a stumble or two: the child can always ask for help on a particular word and then find himself securely back on the page reading, and I hope, having fun. For poetry and learning are both fun and children are full of an enormous relish for both.

I Met a Crow

Said a crow in the top of a tree,
"What time is it getting to be?
    If it isn't yet noon
    I got here too soon,
But I'm late if it isn't yet three."

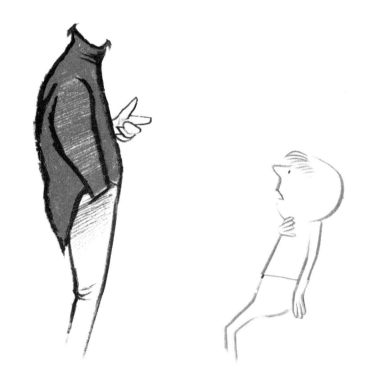

The Man That Had No Hat

I met a man that had no hat,
And when I asked him, "Why is that?"
He looked at me (I think) and said,
"Where should I put it? I have no head."

With that he bowed and went away.
I'm just as glad he didn't stay.
What fun do you think it would be to play
With someone that had no head and no hat?
What fun do you think there could be in that?

The Sleepy Man

I met a man that looked about
As sleepy as he could be without
Falling over and starting to snore.

If he ever wakes up, I'll tell you some more.

This Man Talked About You

I met a man that said he knew
Why the sky is green, why trees are blue,
Why kittens *caw*, and why crows *mew*,
And why the very best one is YOU.

—But kittens don't *caw!* Crows don't *mew!*
The sky is not green! Trees are not blue!

—Yes, I told him that. And he said he knew.
But still, I think, it is just as true
As what he told me about you!

A Man in the Woods Said:

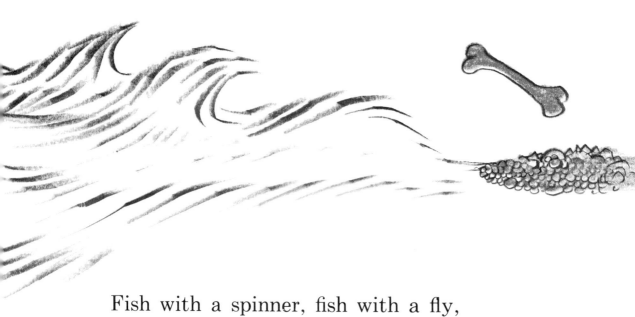

Fish with a spinner, fish with a fly,
Fish when the water is low or high,
But don't try to fish when the lake runs dry.

The Man That Had Little to Say

I met a man at one o'clock who said "Hello"
    at two.
At three o'clock he looked at me and said,
    "How do you do?"
At ten-to-four he said "Good-by" and started
    on his way.
I'm glad he came to see me but he hadn't
    much to say.

The Man That Lived in a Box

I met a man that lived in a box.
His wig was as red as the tail of a fox.
His nose was as long as a fishing rod
(A small one, you know). He grinned like a
    cod,
And nodded his head and looked about
When he popped the lid and came jumping
    out.
And he winked a wink when I put him back
And shut the lid and said, "Goodnight, Jack!"

When I Went to Get a Drink

I said to a bug in the sink,
"Are you taking a swim or a drink?"
    "I," said the bug,
    "Am a sea-going tug.
Am I headed for land, do you think?"

"What a silly!" I said. "That's no sea—
It's a sink!" —"A sink it may be.
    But I'd sooner I think
    Be at sea in the sink
Than sink in the sea, sir," said he.

Have You Met This Man?

Have you met this man? He has no head.
He has no house, but he stays in bed.
He is not too small, he is not too big.
He has no arms, but he knows how to dig.
He cannot swim, yet he goes to sea
Without a boat. Who can he be?

If he knew how, he would say, "I am
No other, sir, than MR. CLAM."

This Man Came From Nowhere

I took a lump of clay in my hand
And patted and pricked it and pulled it AND
There was a man!—with a bump of a head
And two long legs! He winked and said:
"You forgot my ears. You forgot my nose.
You forgot my hands. And, I suppose,
I could think of other things you forgot,
But I don't mind, for I like you a lot,
And I'm glad as can be that you made me this
    way
Out of nothing at all but a lump of clay.
Now try another, and see if you can
Make not just *some,* but *all* of a man."

This Man Went Away

I met a man that was all mine.
He was round and thin and all a-shine.
He had no feet, but he came to me.
He had one eye, but he couldn't see.
He had no fingers, he had no thumb,
But still he gave me a stick of gum.

And then he was gone. He was mine no more,
And I went home alone from the store.

If you want to know who he is, ask Jenny:
She gave him to me.

 —Yes, A BRAND NEW PENNY!

I Met a Man That Was Trying to Whittle

I met a man that was trying to whittle
A ship from a stick, but little by little
The ship he whittled grew littler and littler.
Said he with a sigh, "I'm a very bad whittler!
I've whittled my ship till it's small as a boat.
Then I whittled a hole in it—how will it
    float?"
So he threw it away and cut his throat.
And when he saw his head was gone,
He whittled another and put that on.

The Man in the Onion Bed

I met a man in an onion bed.
He was crying so hard his eyes were red.
And the tears ran off the end of his nose
As he ate his way down the onion rows.

He ate and he cried, but for all his tears
He sang: "Sweet onions, oh my dears!
I love you, I do, and you love me,
But you make me as sad as a man can be."

"Why are you crying," I asked. And he
Stopped his singing and looked at me.
"I love my onions, I do," he said,
"And I hate to pull them out of bed.
And wouldn't it make *you* want to weep
To eat them up while they're still asleep?"

"Then why don't you wake them?"
                                        "Ah," he said,
"Onions are best when they're still in bed!"
And he cried and he ate and he ate and he
        cried
Till row by row and side to side
He ate till there were no more, then sat
And started to cry again for that.

He cried till his coat and shoes were wet.
For all I know, he is crying yet.

I Met a Man That Lived in a House

I met a man that lived in a house
With a cat, and a dog, and a bird,
    and a mouse,
And a big gold fish, and a little brown
    louse.

Said the dog to the cat to the mouse to the
    bird
To the fish to the man, "Have you heard?
    Have you heard?
There's a louse in the house!" Said the louse
    not a word.

Said the man to the fish to the bird to the cat
To the mouse to the dog to his wife, "Think
    of that!
There's a louse in the house and he's there on
    your hat!"

Said the wife to the man to the fish to the
    mouse
To the cat to the dog to the bird, "A louse!
What is he doing here in my house?"

Said the man to the fish, bird, mouse, dog, cat
(And so to his wife), "He is there on your
    hat."

Said the wife to the man to them all, "Think
of that!"

"Think of that!" said the man to the fish to
the bird
To the mouse to the cat to the dog, "Have
you heard?
It's there on her hat!" Said the louse not a
word.

He walked till he came to the end of the hat,
Then he walked on the wife, and he walked
after that
On the bird, on the mouse, on the dog, on the
cat,

On the man, on the fish. He'd be walking
there yet
But he fell off and drowned. —Now don't you
forget:
If you walk on a fish, you may get your feet
wet!

I Met a Man I Could Not See

I met a man I could not see.
But I know he lives not far from me
Out past the lake, and up the hill,
For when the wind and the birds are still,
I stand alone and call "COME OUT!"

And down from the hill I hear him shout:
"OUT! OUT! OUT! OUT! OUT! OUT! OUT! OUT!"

—Well, it *starts* as a shout, as I think you see,
But gets small, and then smaller, then small as can be.
But you can't hear the smallest he knows how to
    say,
For it jumps up the hill and goes far far away

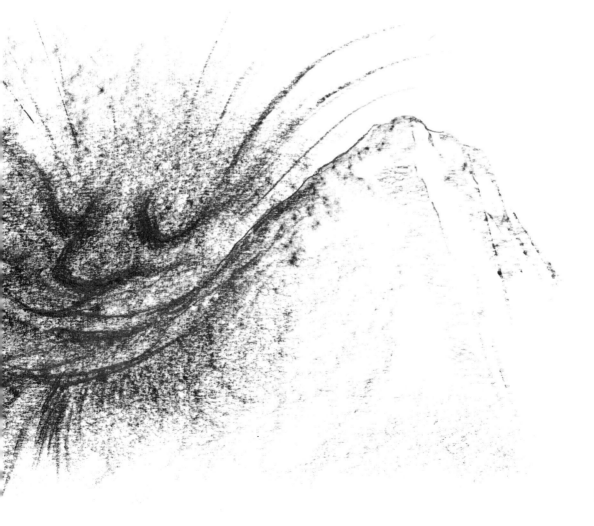

Till it dims into nothing and fades into sky.
And you still *seem* to hear it, far out and up
   high,
Till little by little you hear it grow still,
And you'd say there was no one up there on
   the hill.

But you know that there is. And he's someone
   you know.
And his name is—— That's right! He is
   MR. ECHO.

Then I Met Another Man I Could Not See

Another man I could not see
Called my name from the top of a tree.
And I saw the tree-top bend and sway
As he sang "Come away! Come away! Come
    away!
We shall swing on the tree tops up the hill,
Then flip-flop down like Jack and Jill!
We shall bend the wheat! We shall shake the
    sea!
Come away! Come away! Come away with
    me!"

I stayed where I was, but he ran on
Till the trees fell still and I knew he was gone.
But it's fun to think of him up in a cloud
Whirling and skipping and calling out loud.
Or down by the lake playing tag with the
    trees.

And what may his name be? Well, if you
    please,
Some say MR. WIND, and some say
    MR. BREEZE.

I Met a Man With Three Eyes

I met a man that was very wise.
He had no hands, but he had three eyes,
One green, one yellow, and one red.
He had nothing at all but eyes in his head.
He looked at me and kept winking and
    winking
As if to say, "Guess what I'm thinking."

—You're making it up! It isn't so!

—Oh, yes it is. He is someone you know.
He lives on my street, and he can't talk
But he knows how to say STOP, GO, and
    WALK.
And that's all he says, all day and all night.

—Oh, now I know! —MR. TRAFFIC
    LIGHT!

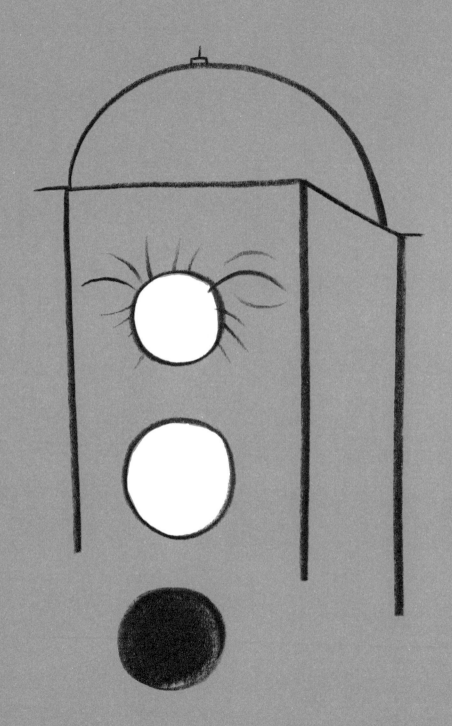

This Man Had Six Eyes!

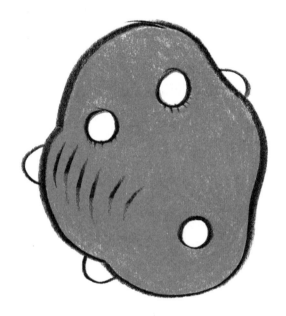

I met a man that had six eyes
And still he could not see.
He lay in bed and hid his head
And would not look at me.

I pulled him up and took him home
(I don't think I did wrong).
And I let him stay, and day by day
I saw his eyes grow long.

I saw them grow out of his head.
I saw them turn to me.
I saw them grow a foot or so.
And *still* he could not see.

"I think he could see the sun," I said,
So I put him on the sill,
And gave him a drink. But what do you
     think?—
His eyes kept growing still.

They grew as long as I was tall.
They grew like a sleepy tree.
They grew to the floor and out the door.
And still they could not see.

Now what do you think has eyes that long?
You may tell me now if you know.
Or look in the pot: there, like as not,
You will find MR. POT 8 OH!

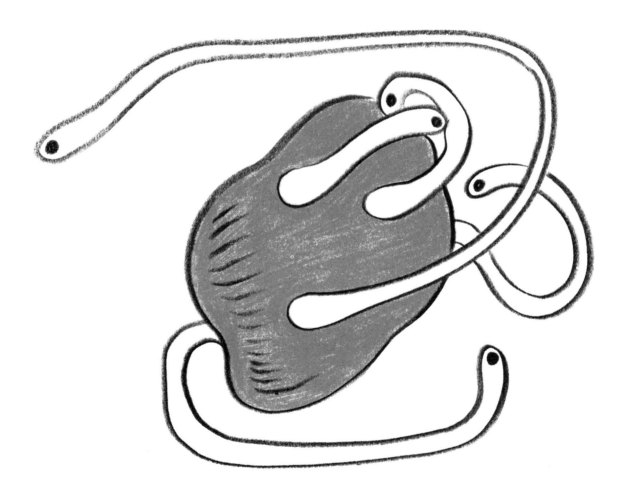

The Cat Heard the Cat-Bird

One day, a fine day, a high-flying-sky day,
A cat-bird, a fat bird, a fine fat cat-bird
Was sitting and singing on a stump by the
  highway.
Just sitting. And singing. Just that. But a
  cat heard.

A thin cat, a grin-cat, a long thin grin-cat
Came creeping the sly way by the highway to
   the stump.
"O cat-bird, the cat heard! O cat-bird scat!
The grin-cat is creeping! He's going to jump!"

—One day, a fine day, a high-flying-sky day
A fat cat, yes, that cat we met as a thin cat
Was napping, cat-napping, on a stump by the
   highway,
And even in his sleep you could see he was a
   grin-cat.

Why was he grinning? —He must have had a
    dream.
What made him fat? —A pan full of cream.
What about the cat-bird? —What bird, dear?
I don't see any cat-bird here.

This Man Lives at My House Now

I met a man on my way to town.
He was spinning up, he was spinning down.
He was twice as red as the nose of a clown.

He took my hand as soon as we met,
And he said to me: "Now don't forget:
I'll spin and I'll spin and I'll spin for you.
I'll spin as fast as you want me to.
For I can spin up and I can spin down.
I can spin all the way to town."

And that's what he did till I told him to stop.
Can you guess his name?

      —Is it MR. TOP?

He's a good spinner.

      —Well, yes, so-so.

But he can't spin up and down. Oh no.
The man I met is called—MR. YOYO!

I Met a Man That Showed Me a Trick

I met a man that showed me a trick.
He said to me, "My name is NICK,
Or PETE, or SAM. You may take your pick."

"Well, then," I said to him, "I'll pick NICK."

So he took out a box and gave me some bread,
And milk, and jam, and when I had fed,
He picked up the box and sighed and said,
"Good-by, I'm going home to bed."

And off he went. (If you guessed the trick,
This is the way you can always trick NICK.
And when you do, you'll have a PICNIC.)

I Met a Man That Was All Head

I met a man that was all head.
He was fat as the moon but redder than red.
He had no ears. He had no chin.
And the rest of him was so long and thin
That it looked to me like nothing but string.

—You're making it up. There isn't a thing
As thin as that!
                    —Yes, there is so.
He was out by the roses. I saw him go
Strolling along with his head held high,
And he nodded to me as he went by.
So I asked his name when I saw him stop
To smell a rose. And he said—POP!

—Well, where did he go? He isn't there.
And he couldn't just sink into thin air!

—Oh, yes he could! as you may see
If you guess his name. What could it be?
I'll give you three hints: he was fat as the
    moon,
And red as a yoyo, and bright as a spoon.
Now do you know? He was MR. BALLOON!

Guess

ONE is a creeper and sleepy in his shell.

TWO is a hopper and he hops very well.

THREE is a flopper and his flippers flap.

FOUR is a jumper with a jump-in lap.

FIVE is a drinker with a dip-in nose.

SIX is a dipper with flippers on his toes.

SEVEN is a tapper with a tripper in his beak.

EIGHT is a nutter with a nut-sack in his cheek.

NINE is a hanger with a banger in his head.

TEN is The Stopper who stepped in and said:

"It's time for the guessing. Here in a line

Are all the numbers from one to nine.

Now look about you, and right or wrong

Guess, if you can, where they belong."

1
2
3
4
5
6
7
8
9
10

I Met a Man Right Here on the Pad

I met a man right here on the pad
I got for my birthday from Mother and Dad.

They gave me a pen, too. And what do you
    think?—
It was I who put him there. And in *ink!*

But he came out very short and stout.
And he had no neck. And his nose stuck out
About as far as an ELEPHANT'S snout.

Well, that wouldn't do. I inked him out

And started again. But his nose hooked out
As big as this:

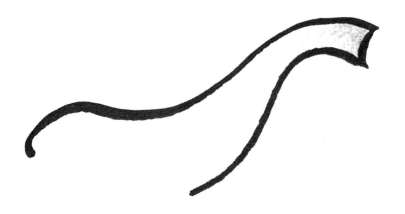

So I made it a spout.
Then I filled him with water—like this, do you see?

Then I put him on, and we all had tea!

The Other Day When I Met Dick

The other day when I met Dick
He said, "I think I'm feeling sick.
A little while back I was feeling fine
And eating my breakfast. I ate nine

Helpings of ham, and ten of fish,
And some of the meat on my Daddy's dish,
And a tub or two of the best wheat flakes,
And another tub of hot pancakes.
Then I ate a pan full of buns with jam,
And another helping or two of ham.

My, I felt fine!

   —But here I am,
Just a little bit later, and as you see,
As sick as a dog. What *can* it be?
I wish I knew what was doing it.
Do you think it would help if I ate a bit?"

I Met a Man That Was Coming Back

I met a man that was coming back.
Where from?
        From putting a THING in a sack.
What THING?
        The THING he was bringing back
From wherever he'd been.
                Well, didn't he say?
Say what?
        What it WAS!
                I didn't stay

To ask him that. I heard the THING
He had in the sack begin to sing:
"Put in another one! *This* one will do!"

And you think the THING in the sack meant
*   you?*

From the look of that man, I'd say it did.
But I ran back of the house and hid.
So he went away with the THING on his
    back.
It was singing away inside the sack:
"Put in another one! Oh, please do!"
—And the last I saw, they were looking for
    YOU!

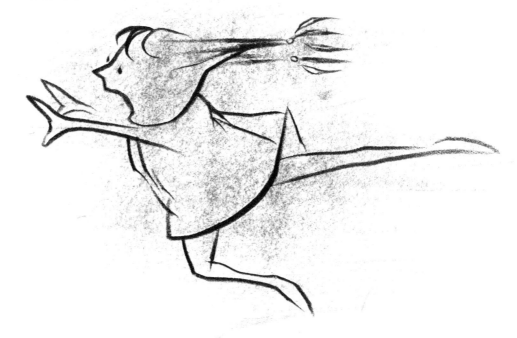

I Wish I Could Meet the Man That Knows

I wish I could meet the man that knows
Who put the fly on my daddy's nose
When my daddy was taking a nap today.
I tried to slap that fly away
So Daddy could sleep. But just as my hand
Came down to slap him, the fly jumped, AND

I hit with a bang—where do you suppose?—
SMACK ON THE END OF DADDY'S
NOSE!

"Ow!" cried Daddy, and up he jumped.
He jumped so hard that he THUMP-
BUMPED
His head on the wall.
Well, I tried to say,
"See, Daddy, I slapped the fly away."
And I should think he would have thanked me.
But what do you think he did? He
SPANKED me!

"I was just trying to help!" I said.
But Daddy was looking very red.
"For trying to help, I have to thank you.
But for that smack on the nose, I'll spank
you!"
And up in the air went his great big hand
As he said, "I hope you understand
It's my nose I'm spanking for, not the fly.
For the fly I thank you."

And that is why
I wish I could meet the man that knows
Who put the fly on my daddy's nose.
For when I find him, I want to thank him.
And as I do, I want to spank him.

I Met a Man Down in the Well

I saw a man down in the well.
What he was doing, I couldn't tell.
But there he was when I went for a drink,
And he looked at me as dark as ink.

He looked up and I looked down,
And he shook his head into a frown.

"What are you looking for down there?"
I shouted. And all he said was—A I R !
And the way he said it, it seemed to come
Out of the well as big as a drum!

"There's no air there, as you should know!"
But all he said to that was—N O !

"Then what do you want? You needn't
    shout!"
And that time all he said was—O U T !

"Come on then. Shall I give you a hand?"

He grinned at me and shouted—A N D!

"And what?" I said. "I wish I knew!"
He shook and he shook and he shouted—
    Y O U!

It was loud as a gun, and I jumped for fear,
But I shouted back: "Now you see here—

I'll bet you think you gave me a fright!"
And up from the well he shouted—R I G H T!

"I'll call my daddy," I said, "and he—"
He shook three times and said—H E! H E!
    H E!

So I dumped a stone down on his head.
And the very last thing he ever said

As the stone came down on him with a crash
Was ——————————————— S P L A S H!

I Met a Man That Had Two Birds

I met a man that had two birds
And a little box all full of words,
And on the box it said THE GAME.

"THE GAME?" said I. "But what's its
    name?"

"Oh," he said to me, "haven't you heard?
It's called LET'S FIND THE BIRDY-
    WORD."

"The Birdy-Word?" said I. "What's that?"

So he put down the box, and then he sat,
And the birds flew down and lit on his hat.
"These are my birds. They play the game.
Take a good look: their tails are the same,
But not their heads."

                    "Do they have a name?"

"I call them WING and DING," he said.
"They are twins in the tail, but not in the head.
And WING and DING—do you see?—are
    words

That are twins at the end — like my two
    birds —
But not at the start. When words do that,"
He said (and the birds jumped on his hat),
"They seem to jig and clap in time.
And when they do *that,* we say they
    R H Y M E.

And that's the game. My little Wing-bird
Jumps into the box and picks a word.
Then Ding takes out one word at a time
Until he finds one that will R H Y M E.

WING   DING

As soon as he sees the right word, Wing
Shakes for joy and begins to sing.
So all day long, one word at a time,
Wing and Ding sing when they R H Y M E.
And that is how they pass the day!''

"That's a grand game. May I see them play?''

"Why, yes, if you like.'' And he said to Ding,
"Are you set to start? Are *you* set Wing?
All right then—GO!'' And out of the box
Ding picked a word, and it was F O X.
Then he flew up to the funny man's hat
While Wing flew down, and there he sat
While the words came up: THING. BRING.
      PING. FLING.
But Ding just sat, for he could not sing
Until the word that came out of the box
Was one that R H Y M E D, as it should, with
      F O X.

BRICK. CLICK. FLICK. THICK. TRICK.
      TICK. CLOCK . . . CLOCKS!

When he had that word, Wing flew from the
      box
And gave the word to his playmate Ding,
And they shook and shook and began to sing.

. . . Would *you* like to play? I have no bird.
And I have no box. But I'll pick a word,
And you keep saying one word at a time.
And as soon as you say one that makes a
      R H Y M E,
We'll shake and shake and start to sing,
And we shall be happy as WING and DING!

I Met a Man That Was Playing Games

—I met a man that was playing games.

—What kind of games?

　　　　　　　　—About things and names.

—How do you play?

　　　　　　　—He didn't say.

But from what I heard, it goes this way:

I pick a rhyme—let's say it's "any"—

If I say "Spend it," you say *penny.*

If I say "Girl," then you say *Jenny.*

If I say "Boy," then you say *Kenny.*

—Yes, I see. May I pick one now?

—What do you pick?

　　　　　　　—Well, I'll pick "how"

And I say "Milk it."

　　　　　　　—I say *cow.*

—I say "It's right here."

　　　　　　　—Then it's *now.*

penny.

Jenny.

Kenny

—I say "It hurts."

—*Ouch!* . . . I mean *Ow!*

—That's right. Your turn now. This game's
    fun.

—I'll make it fast, for I have to run

To meet a man. If I pick "had"

And say "He's mine," then he's . . .

—Your *dad!*

—Right! He's coming on the train.

After supper let's play again!

I Met a Man That Said, "Just Look!"

I met a man that said, "Just look!"—
Here we are at the end of the book!
Think back to all the men you've met.
We'd like to think you won't forget
The things we did and the things we said.
We want you to keep us in your head.

For when you have met us in a book,
You can always find us if you look.
We are here, we are there, we are everywhere:
Far out to sea, high up in the air,
Or in the wind when it blows your hair.
Just look in your head and you'll find us there.

And now, if you please, we are all so glad
You have learned to read (What fun you've
    had!),
We'd like you to play just one last game
With our last man, who says his name

Is MR. IN-AND-OUT. And this
Is all I shall say, for — here he is:

How do you do? I am glad to know you.
And now, if you please, I should like to show
    you

A game I think you may like, my friend.
It's called JUMP-TO-THE-OTHER-END.
And it's played this way:

                If I say LOW

The other end, as you should know,
Is HIGH. Jump to it! Do you see?
Or try another. If I say HE
You jump-to-the-other-end and say SHE.
Or I say LIVE. Jump fast, and try

HIGH

To land, at the other end, on—DIE!

Now shall we try some jumps that go
To words that some of you may not know?

I know you can jump from LIKE to HATE.
But try a good long jump from LATE
To—that's right—EARLY! (That's hard to
    spell.
But not too hard. Just look at it well.)

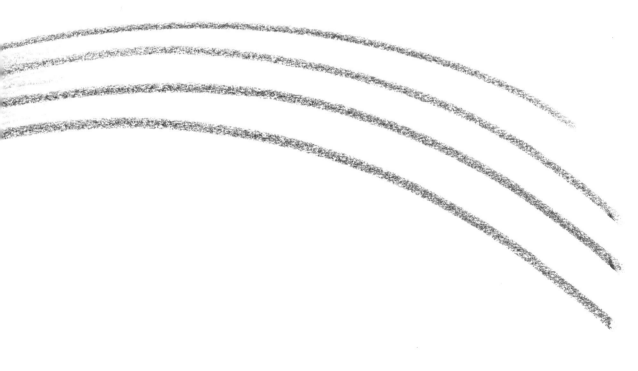

LOW

FORGET

Now jump from FORGET, and where should
   you land?
Yes, on REMEMBER! (Look hard at it and
REMEMBER it.)
                Now then, if you'll take
A very small jump from MEND to BREAK,
And then another from ILL to WELL,
And then one more from BUY to SELL,
You may jump from SOLD!

REMEMBER

—I hope you got
All the way from there to BOUGHT.
For BOUGHT is a word you know how to say,
But think of it being *spelled* that way.
It *sounds* like BOT. But you see it's not.
It's one of those words you have to be
    TAUGHT,
And learning them takes a lot of THOUGHT.
But if you like to learn, you OUGHT
To try and REMEMBER.

—But my it's late!
And we haven't yet jumped from CROOKED
    to—STRAIGHT!
(Did you make that jump? I knew you could!)

—Good-by. You have all been very good,
But I have to go. I shall come and play
With all of you some other day.
REMEMBER my name: MR. IN-AND-OUT.
Look for me please: I'm always about.
Whenever you jump, you'll hear me shout:
"Good for you, my jumping FRIEND!"

—And now it is time to jump to—

THE END